EASY

A FERRO FAMILY STORY

H.M. WARD

H.M. WARD PRESS

LAREE BAILEY PRESS

First Edition: June 2017

ISBN: 9781630350802 (paperbacks)

ISBN: 9781630350796 (ebook)

EASY

VOLUME 1

CHAPTER 1

My life is a lie. Terror courses through me at the thought of someone discovering my secret before I have a chance to figure things out, before I know for certain what happened that night. I can admit it, I ran like a coward and didn't look back. No one expects me to be down here in the dust bowl of the forsaken, in the middle of Texas.

Three months have passed in startling silence since I left New York behind. There's been no trace, no trail, nothing that points to this safe haven. Reporters haven't figured out the girl they've been trailing in Manhattan isn't me. Thank God.

Down here, I've kept my head down and refused invitations to hang out and be a normal twenty-five-year-old, but tonight everything is spinning out of control. The email was waiting for me at work this evening. It's as if the sender knew I'd be working late. Alone.

Four simple words make my heart slam into my chest. The air is ripped from my lungs as I stare at the glowing computer screen.

I KNOW YOUR SECRET.

CHAPTER 2

error courses through my veins while my gaze is locked on the computer screen. I was so careful. How did someone figure it out? Tears sting my eyes, and I swat them away with the back of my shaking hand. Breathing becomes harder, shallow and jagged.

Ice crawls up my spine, and the sensation of eyes watching me makes me shift in my chair. I refuse to glance around, to fall into hysteria. There are no cameras in my office, no bugs on the landline. I check. Frequently. Hell, I don't even use that phone. I don't use my real name. No one knows I'm Jocelyn Ferro.

This threat had to originate in New York. The main problem is that this guy has my work email address. It's not an idle threat. I work at a University that is very easy to find. The ramifications spiral through my mind and crawl across my skin.

My phone lights up and buzzes loudly. The noise throws me further into panic. For a second, I think it's going to say, *UNKNOWN CALLER*. But it doesn't say that.

LIZZIE CUNNINGHAM

The name flashes before me as the cell phone rings a second time, requesting a FaceTime chat.

My heart slows a little and I take another pull of air, trying to steady my facial features before answering. She can't know that I'm rattled. Lizzie thinks I went nuts and ran away, but a best friend like her is too polite to verbalize those thoughts.

All the same, I see it in her eyes when we talk. It might be a different throw-away cell phone, but she's got the same crinkle in the center of her forehead, the one that slightly lifts her brow that lets me know how she feels whether she says it or not. Disapproval. She doesn't think I needed to run. But that's based on what she assumes occurred that night. She doesn't know the truth. No one does, not even me. In the end, it doesn't matter what I do because Lizzie sides with me. Like always. She's the sister I never had.

I swipe the screen and her face appears before coming into focus. She snaps her gum and grins at me. "Hey, girl." She cocks an eyebrow with a swift tilt of her head. A dark lock of hair falls over her shoulder. Before I can greet her, she leans toward her screen and uses a voice that demands an answer, "What's wrong." It's not a question, not really. Her green eyes lock with mine, warning me that bullshit won't be tolerated.

A fake smile finds my face and slithers across it. It's the Ferro way. Hide everything. Always hold it together, no matter what. "I'm fine. I just—"

She cuts me off, her face suddenly filling the entire frame of the screen. If she were standing before me, she'd be close enough to get caught in the splash zone of rapid firing words and spittle. Her voice is hushed, threatening. "You're not fine." She enunciates the final word sharply.

"Lizzie—"

"I can see it all over your face. You don't think I know

you? Fuck that, Jos. I do, and something is very wrong! I'll be there are soon as you say the word. Tell me where you've been hiding and I'll be there with the jet. I'll fix this, Jos. It'll be all right."

I try to interrupt again, "Liz—"

Shaking her head sharply, she pulls the phone far enough back that I can see her finger flying as she speaks. It's the Italian in her. "I'll take care of anyone who fucks with you. No one messes with you, not while I'm around." She practically growls the last few words.

My plastic Ferro façade cracks at her protectiveness. I smile again, but it's the sad brokenness that I feel mixing with a death wish that pulls the corners of my mouth up into a mournful crushed hope of an expression. "Someone made me. He knows."

Lizzie's tiger sneer softens as her eyes widen. "Who?"

"I don't know. I was finishing up work—"

She rolls her eyes. "Oh God, you and the job. You're the only billionaire heiress who works. I told you I'd send you more money."

"Lizzie." I snap without meaning to. My jaw falls open as I search for words. This defeat feels like a heavy foot on my chest. Someone outplayed me and I didn't see it coming. There were no clues at all.

Everything about my life in Texas is fake, but I have a feeling that's not what this email is talking about. I'm sure they know I'm here—this was sent to my work email address. There's only one secret that I guard even closer, because if they find out what I've done... My skin crawls. I don't even want to finish the thought.

I rant, spelling out every worry running through my mind until sobs cling to the top of my throat. I tug at my hair with one hand and try not to cry. "I fucking hacked my hair off and colored it crayon-red! I used the best guy to make fake IDs and paid him to keep his mouth shut. If it was him, he'd ask for more money."

Lizzie breaks in, "There's no way it was him. He wouldn't fuck with the Ferros. He'd rather have you as a client anyway."

"Then who is it? Has anyone figured out what we did?"

The Kool-Aid hair-do helped disguise me but I still have the Ferro features. Thank God I didn't get the blue eyes. People never remember that Bryan and I were the only Ferro children born with emerald green orbs instead of the sapphire hue that is as dominant as the Ferro nose. Thankfully, I had that Italian schnoz taken care of when I was younger. Graduation present. Or demand. It depends on how you look at it. Mother was insistent that we make my profile more feminine to match the nose Aunt Constance and mom had created. It presents an air that everything is real, even Ferro plastic surgery. No one knew about it. I simply vanished from society and when I reappeared my nose was slimmer and the bridge was lowered, sharp angular lines still intact.

"What's been going on up there? Did they figure it out yet?"

"No one realizes what we did, Jos." She leans back into a posh lime-green sofa that's located in her bedroom in Manhattan. Her hand runs through her long dark locks, pushing the soft curls away from her face. My hair was just like hers until twelve weeks ago.

"Are you certain? It's been longer than we expected and no one's noticed I'm missing?"

"Right," she snaps, pressing her hand to her ample chest, offended. "I didn't blow my cover. Everyone still thinks I'm you."

"How is that possible? That lie shouldn't have held together this long."

Lizzie snorts a dark laugh. "People see what they want to see. Dumb assholes with cameras glued to their faces, and your parents don't care as long as you don't shame them. I showed up at your house last night, tossed your bedding around to make it look like you finally spent a night at home, and no one looked for you. Not your parents or your brothers. No wonder why you couldn't stand it anymore."

I swallow hard. That's the truth, the cold hard facts. The only one who cared about me is in the ground and I stole the happiness he could have had because of fucking Ferro rules. I'm a traitor. The worst kind.

CHAPTER 3

*A*fter a moment, I release a shaky breath. "I don't want to talk about any of that. I need to figure out who made me. If it's someone up there or someone new down here."

"It could be someone down there. Did you fuck anyone? Angry ex, maybe?"

Annoyed with her, I glare at the screen and respond calmer than I feel. "No, nothing like that. I've kept to myself. I told you." She doesn't know the half of it. I'm a fucking hermit, save this job. For a girl who breathes people like air, being alone so often has been exhausting.

"Maybe it's your Dad?"

Tensing, I swallow hard. After a moment, I ask, "Did he say anything that makes you think that?"

Lizzie thinks for a moment and then shakes her head. "No, but you know how he is and you know what he'd do if he found out. That man has no fucking clue. About anything."

I remember. Vividly. Nothing was mine. Father made it

clear that I was an object to be used however he deemed necessary. Most tasks were handed off through my mother, and I had to do whatever she requested. But when a request has no other option but compliance, it's a command. I lived like that for as long as I could.

One night everything went to Hell. That was my mistake. That night broke me. Now I'm here. In Abilene, Texas at this tiny university with blonde bricks and glass buildings. Hiding.

Lizzie shakes her head. "Nah, but he wouldn't be the type to directly come at you, right? I mean if your dad knew, he'd play with you first to make you lose your shit, and then make himself known." She's guessing and doesn't realize the extent of my father's ability to strike terror. There's a reason why the Ferro family has few enemies. His reputation is worse than Aunt Constance in terms of maliciousness and getting anything he wants. I witnessed it firsthand. To have that venom aimed at me is a cringe-worthy thought.

Lowering my gaze, I take a long slow breath of air and release it. I shake my head before looking up at the phone. Still, this is too subtle to be him. Email isn't his style. "No, this isn't Dad. This is too passive to be him."

There's a moment of silence as we both think. Then Lizzie offers, "Tell me where you are and I'll come help you figure it out."

"You can't. Lizzie, we've been over this." I try to hide my frustration because she has gone to great lengths to make sure I pulled this off. No one knows I'm gone and it's because of her. "You can't visit. They'll find me if you come here." I can tell the conversation's derailed. She's been pissed at me for months because I won't tell her everything. It seems to offend her to her core.

"You trust me with everything else, but not this?" I don't

reply. She releases a rush of air through her nose and fogs the screen. It dissipates swiftly. Her expression softens when she realizes I'm not talking. "Jos, at least tell me where you are," she whines as she twirls a lock of hair around her finger. It's something I would have done a year ago.

"You know I can't, and you can't get caught. Where are you?"

She sniffles and straightens her shoulders. "At home. I haven't left yet."

"Where are you going?"

"The usual line-up. Dark clubs, loud music, and all that shit. Jos, you've been gone for months. How much longer do you plan on staying there?" There's an edge to her voice that makes it seem like she's annoyed with me. I don't blame her.

"Sounds good. Stay in the shadows. We look alike, but not that much." We're roughly the same size, build, and height. Her skin tone is more olive than mine. That presented a problem so we came up with a plan where it wouldn't be an issue. It worked better than either of us thought.

She snorts and points to her wig. "The hair hides my non-Ferro face and since our plastic surgery doc was a dick and gave us the same nose, no one notices. Besides, Jos, no one looks at your face. Your dresses look like they were painted on. I had to lose five pounds to get into them."

She lowers the phone to show off one of the Gucci cocktail dresses Mother had commissioned for me. It's retro, something from the 1960's with sections of clear plastic across the under-bust which dips low and spilled down my sides. I felt naked in that thing. The patches of red fabric were soft, but scarce. The hemline was barely to the top of my thigh and the neckline was non-existent. It dipped to my navel in front and showed the small of my back from behind. It was taped on because no dress like that could hold itself in place.

Lizzie loves the dresses that were for ruining some poor fool. My reputation of being easy combined with a dress like that made it difficult for the morally chaste congressman to appear to be doing anything moral. A hand on his arm with enough cleavage revealed and it ruined that guy. I remember him. Mother said he was a problem and that was the extent of the information shared on the subject. I ruined people without knowledge.

My parents think I'm a slut and used my always open legs to their advantage. The truth is, I haven't had sex in months. Actually, it's been nearly a year. The last guy I was with just wanted to brag that he bagged Jos Ferro. There is always that risk. It's painful to never know if the guy liked me or even cared. I let the easy reputation blossom at one point. I didn't care and was trying to drown out my sorrow. It didn't work, but it did set up an easy to follow map of what Jos Ferro does at night, and since I fight with my parents all day—and avoid them as much as possible—nothing seems amiss, yet. Thank God, because I need more time.

"That dress looks great on you," I offer. Lizzie preens as she represses a smile of gratitude. "I'll be home as soon as I can. Be careful. Don't get caught."

"I won't. I've got your back for as long as you need." Although her face is completely sincere, there's a tired timber in her voice that says she's wearing thin—that she can't do this much longer. "Your parents are being a bunch of little shits, but I have them under control. Maybe the email was from your mother? That's unlikely, but I can go over there and poke around. Find out what shit is brewing in the Ferro mansion."

"That's a good idea." I pause, and then joke, "And make sure you go over as you. As clueless as my parents are, I think they'd recognize that you're not their daughter."

She cackles and presses a hand to her heart. "Seriously—

no worries. I'll check in with you if I find out anything. Otherwise, watch your back. Love ya, bitch."

I smile and laugh slightly. "Love you, too." Before I can say be careful again, she's gone.

CHAPTER 4

I shove the phone in my purse and shut off the computer. I need a techie to trace where this email came from, but if I show the email to anyone it'll raise questions. Irritation prickles down my spine. Every time I talk to Lizzie it becomes clear that I've made no progress. I still don't know what to do or how I can fix things so I can go home. The email means I'm out of time.

I grab my bag and shut off the lights to my broom closet of an office and head down the darkened halls. I'm lost in thought, not even realizing that I'm passing by the one place on campus that I can't resist—the concert hall.

There is a row of stage lights shining down, casting an amber glow on the edge of the stage and first few rows of chairs. The soft illumination reveals a man standing over a music stand. His hands grip the sides as his head hangs low. I don't recognize him. The school isn't that big, but still, I don't know every face. That's to my benefit because that means most of them don't see me. We're a city of strangers who nod in hallways and walk through life blind, never really looking our fellow man in the face.

The crayon-colored hair is off-putting for many. They see it and can't take me seriously, so they don't bother with pleasantries even if this is the Southwest. I'm an outsider. They sense it and they're right, but it's not the obvious. It never is.

The man lifts a baton and slashes it through the air for a few measures to an invisible orchestra before stiffening. He grips the small piece of wood tightly before hurling it across the wooden stage floor. His other hand swipes the pages and the sheet music goes flying. He clutches the sides of the music stand firmly. His back arches as it fills with air and every muscle in a strong body tightens.

I know how he feels. I walk away. I can't help anyone. I can't even help myself. What good would I be to him? A weight settles heavily across my shoulders and sinks into my chest. I've been here for ninety days and I'm no better for it. I could pick up and run again—go somewhere else and hide. The problem I've noticed is something I don't want to face. Not tonight.

You just need more distance, Jos, a voice chimes softly in the back of my mind.

I'm starting to think that she's wrong. I'm two-thousand miles from home in a place that makes no sense to me. The people here are super religious but only on Sunday mornings and Wednesday nights. It's like they're living a double life and it doesn't concern them in the least. They don't even see it. It's Jesus this and Godly that, but they'd cut a mofo for taking their parking spot at the local WalMart after services. At least the plastic people in Manhattan know they're fake. Maybe I don't see it because faith eludes me, but if living like that is what it means to believe in God, I can't do it. I lie enough for my parents. I don't need another all-powerful, self-centered asshat telling me what to do. I have enough of that at home.

I head out of there as fast as I can and don't think too hard about where I'm headed. Dark, noisy, alcohol. No one will recognize my voice with the banjo twanging or the boots sliding. And I sure as hell need a drink tonight. The thought of going home alone right now scares me. *Maybe I should jump in my car and keep driving.* Maybe that thought was a premonition. Either way, I didn't listen and staying changed everything.

CHAPTER 5

When I get to the bar, I shun every guy who tries to pick me up. That email has me on edge and I practically bite the head off of every man brave enough to approach. I down another shot and slam it on the bar top.

The barkeep is a young guy with dark skin and thick arms. He's got a shaved head with a tattoo across the back of his neck. The collar on his white shirt hides the details, but there's a bit of ink peeking above the edge of the fabric. He glances at me but says nothing. He's been keeping an eye on the guys who come up and get shot down. I gave him the last set of drinks two guys sent over—as if I'd jump into bed with two men.

I sigh deeply as I try to get the persistent cowboy on the stool next to me to go away. I'm scrolling through a news feed and not listening to him when he places a hand on my thigh and rolls his wrist so his fingertips brush the V at the top of my legs. I jump out of my chair and scream, "What the fuck!"

The guy is wearing a huge ass white felt cowboy hat with a plaid shirt and very tight ironed jeans. Coupled with the boots, he's one of those pretty frat boy cowboys—not the actual working cowboy that comes in dusty from working hard on a farm all day. His face is impish with a nose that is two sizes too large. His eyes are small and beady like a rodent.

He remains seated and flicks his thumb to the back of his nose and laughs at me. "Calm down, honey. I'll buy you a drink first if that's the way you want it." He chortles in a light, airy way that makes me irate.

"Go fuck yourself," I growl. People are watching us now and my anger has sharpened my accent. It's clear I'm not one of them, that I'm a Yankee city girl. I've seen how they treat other women when they realize she's not from a small town. It's awful, but I'm too angry to care at the moment. My body is tense, every muscle corded tight, as my left-hand balls into a fist at my side.

"Now, that's not a very purdy thing to say, sweetheart. You city girls have filthy mouths. I know what I'd like to do with that sinful set of lips." He stands up and is way too close to me. His belt buckle catches on my blouse as he rises. I step back but he moves toward me.

The bartender speaks behind me. "Simmer down, Tommy. She ain't interested."

Tommy glances past me at the guy and grins. "She don't know that, not really. These fast women wander in from the city and bring their trashy ways with 'em. Well, it's our patriotic duty to show them what a real Texan woman would do. It gives her something to aspire to."

When he redirects his attention toward me, he's all slimy smiles, arrogance, and asshole. The guy never sees my fist coming until it connects with his cheek. I throw all my weight into it and slam straight into his jaw. It gives under my knuckles as the look of shock on his face suddenly turns to anger. The place has gone quiet, everyone watching, too afraid to blink because they'll miss what happens next. I stand there shaking, staring at the man, ready to punch him again.

A table of college boys jeers the man, humiliating him. "That's not how you pick up a woman, dude!" The table laughs, followed by a few other fellows sitting around the bar. The women don't smile or move. They're still watching us.

Tommy leans down and gets in my face, hissing, "You'll pay for that, bitch."

Before he can say another word, Tommy is yanked away and staggers backward. A strong hand is holding the collar of his shirt. I follow the grip and see it's connected to the man that threw the sheet music in the concert hall. There's nothing soft about him now, no indication that he held a baton less than an hour ago.

He roughly handles Tommy, pulling him close enough to whisper to the man. Tommy's rage drains, leaving his face pale and his eyes wide. His jaw hangs open, apparently intimidated by the quiet threats of the concert hall guy. Tommy rips away from him and staggers back a step. He glares at me before turning on his heel and rushing out.

The college guys burst out laughing. A few pound the table and hurl insults after Tommy. I'm still standing by my stool, heart racing, with clenched fists still ready to fight. The concert hall guy paces toward me, dark boots scuffing the peanut shells as he nears me. I don't want to talk, but I suppose I need to thank him. My lips part, waiting for him to ask if I'm all right, an answer already on my tongue when he sweeps past me and says nothing. He doesn't even look at me. He heads to the end of the bar and takes a seat. A moment later, an amber liquid is placed in front of him by the barkeeper who obviously knows this moody mystery maestro. The man keeps his dark head down, eyes on his drink, and ignores everything else.

Part of me is glad he didn't hit on me, but the rest of me is offended that he didn't ask if I was all right. I sit down on my stool and swallow my thanks. Cowboys are assholes. Or maybe all men are assholes. I can't tell at the moment because this guy is so intense that it's hard to look away. I find myself staring at him.

When he lifts his head, he looks straight past me. It pisses me off so badly, that I down my drink, and saunter over to the end of the bar.

"What's wrong with you?" I demand. I stand next to the stool at his side and glare at his chiseled cheek, dusted with stubble.

He doesn't turn to look at me. He doesn't make any indication that he's aware of me.

"What the hell? Why bother helping me if you're going to be as big a dick as the other guy?"

He laughs. It's a deep sound, surprised almost. He keeps his focus locked on the other end of the bar and remains silent after that brief chortle.

I walk back to my spot, grab my next shot, and then head to the opposite end of the bar. I sit down in the place where the beautiful silent man had been staring. I expect him to look away, but he doesn't. I lift my shot and down the liquid before slamming the glass on the bar. His eyes are ice blue, nearly silver, they're so light. I expected them to be dark. The contrast with his tanned skin and inky hair is striking. He holds my gaze and it feels like a challenge to see who will look away first.

I have no idea what his damage is, but I'm too tired to

deal with crazy guys tonight. I tip up my chin at him and say the one word that I feel I must convey. "Thanks."

When I slide off the stool, I pay my tab, and head for the door. As I shove out into the cool night air, I take a deep breath. That's when the hairs on my arms rise up and connect at the back of my neck. I glance around, seeing no one, but I sense him.

CHAPTER 6

hat Tommy guy is out here. It has to be him. Or maybe it's the email person.

I step off the wooden deck that surrounds the door to the bar and into the gravel parking lot. The crunch of caliche under my feet sounds like airhorns. The night wind kisses my skin as it blows past. The air is never still here.

I head to my car, glancing around, but not seeing him. When I get to my vehicle, I touch the handle and the door unlocks. I got an Elantra that's a few years old. I was driving a Bentley in New York and I feel weird saying it, but I like this car better. Maybe it's because I bought it and it's mine, or maybe it's because I actually like it. I don't know, but I slip into my seat and try to pull the door shut.

Tommy catches it and swings it open. He stands there between the door and me, glaring down. "You made a mistake making an enemy of me tonight."

I have a Taser in my glovebox, but I'm afraid to move. If I lean over, he might climb on top of me and if the man pins me, it won't go well.

I tense and shoot back, "You grabbed my snatch in the

middle of a bar. What did you think was going to happen? It's not a pickup line, asswipe. Go away before I press the panic button and the police show up."

A sneer tugs at the side of his mouth as he leans on the door frame. "They'll get here right after I'm done with you. Go ahead and press it." He lunges for me, and I go for the glove box, diving across the front seats.

He grabs me and pins me across the seat, shoving my back into the gearshift. I try to get a knee up, but can't move. I scream as I claw at him. Panic has made me stupid. My head is by the glove compartment. As the asshole unzips, I push the button and the Taser topples out. Blindly, I turn it on and slam it into his neck when he looks up to see what I've done. His body tenses and then goes still before he's torn off me and dragged backward out of the little car.

That's when another man reaches for me with a strong hand on a thick arm. I don't think. I can't. I just act and press the Taser to his skin. The guy goes down like a bag of bricks. Silence fills the parking lot. I scamper out of the car to see who the second man. Tommy must have planned a gangbang with me as the prize. This had to be an asshole friend that thought he could take advantage of a girl that was clearly out of her element and off-kilter tonight. Well, fuck them.

As I stand, I look down to the second man lying at my feet and swear. It's the concert hall guy. I can't leave him on the parking lot ground with the lunatic cowboy. For all I know, Tommy will wake up first and castrate the man. He doesn't deserve that.

I walk around the pile of limbs and pull out the concert hall guy and lug his heavy body into the back of the car. After wrestling his toned, tall frame into the back seat, I stare at my handiwork. He's not in there too comfortably. Okay, it's bad. He's sort of sitting on his face, but I can't flip him around. He's way too heavy. I was lucky I got him in the damn car. Screw it. I slam the door and leave him sitting on his face.

After starting the engine, I maneuver around the prone cowboy and get the hell out of there. When I stop at a traffic light, I turn to see how the guy in my backseat is doing and come face to face with him. A scream rips from my throat and before I know it, my hand that's still clutching the Taser connects with his neck.

He sees it coming this time and utters, "Don't—"

But I already connected the electrodes to his skin and he slumps to the side.

"Shit!" I repeat the word too many times as a car horn behind me blares. I've been sitting at a green light. I hit the gas and decide to head toward home. I have no idea what I'm going to do with this guy when I get there. He helped me and I Tasered him.

Twice.

Shit.

CHAPTER 7

I'm so frazzled that I don't know what to do. I'm creeping toward my house, following the dark winding farm roads outside of town. The moon sits like a dinner plate against an inky sky. Stars scatter in a thick path like diamonds that fell out of a rich man's pocket. They glitter brightly in the darkness.

Indecision has me paralyzed. The last place I should be taking him is toward my home, but my brain seems to have flipped to autopilot. When I'm freaked out, I run home and hide. Let's just say I'm past the freak-out point. My heart already crawled up my throat and ran down the street. It's in the next town by now, and now I'm a heartless bitch debating whether or not to help a guy I maimed.

I pull into my driveway and crunch up the path that leads to the house, weaving through the property until the street is completely hidden. I throw the car in park and look over my shoulder. Concert Hall Guy's still out, big body sprawled across the back of my car, eyes closed as if dreaming. When he wakes up this guy is going to think I kidnapped him. I debate bringing him inside or leaving him in the car.

Stupidity would tell me to bring him in, or maybe that's compassion. I don't know. The two traits are tangled together at this point. If I invite him inside, the guy might recognize me. Or hell, maybe he's the one who sent the email. Either way, bringing a strange, albeit beautiful man, into my little house would be foolish. The night could still get worse. Opting for a Taser instead of a gun may have been stupid. But, I didn't think I needed one. I never imagined a scenario where I'd want the comfort of holding a strange man at gunpoint while sorting out my night. But Tasing this guy a third time would be cruel. It would suck if the helpful bystander was made impotent by being electrocuted too many times. That would deter any man from helping a woman ever again.

Sighing, I twist in my seat and peer down at the man. Dark lashes rest against tanned skin. Sharp cheekbones flow into a strong jaw. And those lips, they're pink and full and surrounded with the perfect amount of stubble. There are no scars, nothing that says total psycho, but I suppose there is a way to pass the crazy test. After a brief inner debate, I lean over the seatback and reach for him. My hips rest on the center console as I strain my hand and reach into his pocket. Come on, wallet. Where are you? I need to Google this guy before he comes to and thinks I'm molesting him.

Heart racing, I feel a hard bit of leather against the edge of my fingers. I lean closer, wrap my fingers around it, and pull. I remain perched on the console and have his license out before flicking my phone to life. I pull up Google and enter his name. Two seconds later, results appear.

CHASE DESPARAUX. Facebook, Twitter, Tumbler, and a few other social media sites pop up. No newspaper articles that say, WANTED KILLER. Nothing horrible. No devastatingly attractive girlfriend either. A few pictures of him conducting. That's it. It doesn't mean he's kosher, but at least he's not a known murderer.

I pocket my phone and close his wallet. I need to put it back in his pants pocket before he wakes up. I lean forward carefully and inch toward his body. His chest rises and falls slowly, still out. There's a peaceful expression on that hardened face, almost pleasant as I reach for his back pocket again. I try to shove the wallet back in, but he's heavy. The guy is laying on his side, and the weight on his back pocket prevents me from getting the wallet to slip into his pants. One side will slide in freely, but the part closest to the seat won't budge.

Chanting, "Don't wake up, don't wake up," I shove harder and slip my hand under his rump the tiniest bit. My finger tips are on his ass and stuck between this man and the seat.

I glance at him. Even breathing, so he's still out. In the dark, I can't see a damned thing. It's all silhouettes and faint sounds. I don't want this guy to think I Tased him to steal his money. This isn't working. I need to change position, which requires getting out of the car.

I cut the engine and quietly open my door and leave it open. The dome light turns on and brightens things. My pulse pounds in my ears, thinking the light will rouse the man, but no. He's still out. Apparently, it's not as easy to shake off the effects this time.

I slink around to the back door and pull it open before ducking my head inside to try and look behind him. I need to get a better angle on replacing his wallet in his back pants pocket. I can't reach over him. Crawling on him would wake him. I can't really reach from here, not without something to lean on a little. I see a way to reach around him if I place myself on my tippy toes and hold onto the oh-shit strap. It gives me enough room that I should be able to put it back without touching him. I can't believe I'm doing this. Attempt number two. After this I'm going to throw it on the floor and say it fell out.

I'm leaning halfway into the automobile with my feet on the gravel driveway and one hand holding me an inch over the beautiful man while the other arm is extended toward his ass clutching his wallet. I barely breathe as I reach over him, my face close to his back, and try to shift him enough to get the hand holding his wallet up under his ass.

That's when a deep voice says, "If you wanted me that badly, you should have said so at the bar."

I screech and fall. On top of him. My pulse spikes to stroke territory as gravity pulls me down. I flail, possibly punching him in the face as I claw backward and fall out of the car. I yelp with a THUD and drop his wallet somewhere along the way.

Icy Eyes sits up and leans on the car door before he looks down at me. "So, do you always pick up guys like this? Have them break up a fake fight, shove them in the backseat of your car, and then drive out of town and grope their asses?"

"No! I swear to God, this wasn't staged." My hands are on the ground on either side of my hips. Horrified, I frantically shake my head trying to think of something to explain myself that doesn't make his suspicions sound founded. Jaw dangling, I gape and can't find words.

He shrugs. "I mean, it's different. You take the cake in the unique category. I've had girls try and take my shit before, but none ever kidnapped me." He's smirking the entire time he talks, but his tone is serious. He thinks I'm insane. The half-smile fades and he says somberly, "Can I ask you something?"

I nod, still sitting on the ground, looking up at his beautiful face. "What?"

"Is your house made out of gingerbread?" I blink at him. "Do I need to run like hell in that direction?" He jabs his thumb away from my house and toward the field. He glances at the acreage and then back at me, running a hand through his hair and down the back of his neck.

Jaw scraping the ground, I gape at him. Is he joking?

Then he adds, completely dead-pan, "That wouldn't matter anyway, right? I could run, run as fast as I can, but the witch still eats that sucker at the end of the story. Poor bastard." The slight smirk is back, the corner of his mouth rising slightly on one side.

I glare at him. "Did you seriously call me a witch? I could have left you back there." Not that I would have thrown the guy to that lunatic, Tommy. Mr. Handsome aka Gingerbread Man would have ended up dead in a ditch.

He takes a step toward me. Chase. His name is Chase. "I don't think you're that cold."

"You don't know anything about me." I'm firm, even though my ass is still on the ground and he's looking down at me from the backseat with his feet on the gravel drive. He stands.

His eyes sweep over me, taking in my outfit and bright hair. There's no lift to the corner of his lips this time. Again, he shakes his head as he slips his hands into his pockets. "If you're soliciting for being a cold-hearted bitch, then I'm not buying. I see you, no matter what you think." He studies my Kool-Aid cut and then his cool eyes slip over my piercings—ear to eyebrow—before slipping down to my unmanicured nails. His gaze rests on my left hand.

I don't know what he sees, but he thinks he sees something. I'm on my feet and fold my arms over my chest. It looks too defensive, but I don't care. This arrogant man can't know me. If he has the slightest clue who I am, I'm screwed. I laugh, but it's a jaded sound. I press a hand to my chest, flexing the fingers as I do it. "How flattering to be told I'm so transparent."

"You made snap judgments about me. We all do it. The only difference is that I've never been wrong."

I scoff and tighten my folded arms while cocking out my hip. "I'm sure."

He inhales slowly, lashes lowered, as a softness overtakes his features. Hard lines melt away and I feel safe. It's as if I'm seeing his walls drop. The movement has a sensuality to it and I suspect the only other time this man makes that expression is when he's tangled in sheets and covered in sweat. I should look away, but I can't. There's something about him, hypnotic and raw. It keeps me there, eyes fixated on him.

When he finally speaks, his voice is a soft timbre and it lulls like a seduction song. But his words are quite the opposite. They pierce and pull, tug and rip away at me. "There's an incident in your past that you couldn't overcome, or accept. You're scared and alone, but the loneliness is self-afflicted. You shun people who are kind to you and trust isn't something you believe in. There's no such thing as love and you believe that you're beyond hope—beyond saving. You hide beneath that assertive hair, that hard exterior shell you created. You hope to God no one gets past the façade because what lies beneath is so terrifying even you can't face it."

It feels as if I've been struck. My throat tightens as the air is pulled from my body. Defense mode clicks on mid-speech and a flippant smile spreads across my face. My eyes roll to the side a little as a know-it-all smirk reaches my eyes. My body says he couldn't be more wrong, but how did he read me that way…that close. It was a prediction of things to come, but an assessment of things that have already passed.

I laugh and feel my eyes crinkle as a hand finds his shirt. I press my palm lightly to his chest, splaying that hand as the other presses to my heart. I chortle, not looking him in the eye. I don't deny it. That would come across too defensive and make him think he's right. Instead, I do what I've always done and twist the truth into lies. "Let me guess, a failed psych major who still has fun analyzing everything?"

Icy eyes meet mine as a dark brow lifts. "I could keep going or...?" He glances at my hand, still on his chest, lying gingerly on the supple fabric of his shirt.

I hold his gaze and try not to back away from the intensity of it—of him. "Or?"

"Or I could help you."

Bristling, I mutter under my breath, "I don't need help."

He lowers his face to mine and says softly, "No matter what you've been through and what you believe, I won't hurt you. You have my word. I could call an Uber and leave you alone if that's what you want, but that cut is on your right arm and you're right handed. Fixing it up alone will be rough. I know you can do it, but maybe you don't need to push back so hard tonight. Maybe you could make an exception this once?" He inclines his head toward me.

I finally manage to speak, but I find myself parroting back his question "An exception?"

There are no serious wounds on me. What the hell is he talking about? When I look down at my arm, I gasp. There's a long deep cut that I don't remember getting. Ribbons of blood have caked into a burnt color and dried on my arm, but the cut is deep and still wet in the middle, still weeping.

My head feels too heavy and I laugh, even though I want to cry. "I'm fine."

He cocks his head to the side and catches my eyes. Carefully, he reaches out and places a hand on my shoulder. I don't shake him off. His voice is soft, sincere, "Don't send me away. Not yet." He doesn't pull back when I stare at his hand like it's wrong, like the gesture is a mistake—like he's a mistake.

Time unknits in that moment. The franticness evaporates

as I stare at his strong hand, the same one that saved me earlier, the palm of the man I Tasered more than once tonight. For some reason he's still here, still offering me help.

He should have run. I should have shoved him out of the car and into a field.

This friendship can only end in heartache and destruction because that's what it means to be a Ferro. I've watched it happen to my brothers and cousins more times than I can bear. The solace of this place gives me distance to realize that I'm better off alone, that I'll tank anyone kind enough to help me. I know what my family is capable of, and I know they'll disapprove of him.

I also know that a musician in no-where Texas who has the heart of a cowboy but dresses like a city guy makes me wonder. There's a dichotomy inside him and he's not conflicted about it. I want to know how. I want to be able to accept who I am and the choices I've made with such ease. Or maybe I'm so weary and alone that I find my answer has changed from the time I first made up my mind.

The sound tumbles over my lips unexpectedly, making my heart jump. "Okay."

He smiles and adds, "My name is Chase, by the way." I nod, unable to speak, and turn away from him to unlock the door.

CHAPTER 8

*M*y home is a little tiny house on three acres of land just north of the city. I'm halfway between Abilene and Anson with nothing but stars as neighbors. This was intentional when I first moved here. I was infatuated with the solitude and serene nights. I've traveled the world and stayed at the most elite resorts and hotels, but the night sky here compares to none. It blows the Caribbean stars out the water.

The entire milky way glitters across my backyard, and I loved it so much that I made a special modification to the tiny house and had dual skylights installed over the bed in the upper loft. The old Texan warned me about hail and wind, saying it wasn't frugal and that I'd be replacing those panes of glass every time a storm rolled through, but I was in love with the sky and the freedom it offered. I like thinking that I'm small, a grain of sand on a beach, inconsequential. It's so much more devastating when you're important and fail to be everything required. I've failed. Hard.

I unlock the door, and he follows me inside. I'm standing in my hotel-room-sized house with a man who fills half of it.

The outside of the little house has a Norwegian flare with cedar shingles stained gray and overflowing flower boxes under narrow vertical windows trimmed in white. A square wooden deck stands before a cobalt front door flanked with two white chairs.

The first floor has my living room, kitchen, and bathroom while the upper loft holds my bedroom. It literally takes one stride to change rooms, and since I never have any company, my things are out—books, magazines, nail kit, laundry, etc. A dim bulb illuminates when we push inside the room thanks to home automation. I'm off the grid here with generators and solar panels for electricity, rain barrels for the shower, and a compost potty that isn't as nasty as it sounds. I have no internet and no land lines. There's nothing that will ping that this little house even sits here when looking through utility bills. I bought the land with cash, purchased the house the same way, all under an alias. I was careful, so careful.

That's why this one action seems so reckless. I've brought someone to my hiding spot. But I'm already found. My time here is limited. This house will be left behind even though I wish I didn't have to walk away.

My heart hammers into my chest, slapping it silly. I wasn't the type of girl to turn into a hermit and live alone. I love people, the sounds of the city and the way it sings at night, the symphony of sounds on a summer night in Manhattan cannot compare.

Swallowing hard, I glance back at my guest as he closes the door behind him. The intimate space suddenly feels too revealing. Intending to back toward the door to open it again and show him out doesn't go as planned. He doesn't move. His neck cranes as he looks around the tiny home with awe, lips slightly parted, and eyes filled with something I don't recognize. It can't be wonder. Shock, maybe?

Either way, wonder and shock are knocked out of him when I slam into him, butt first followed by a sharp elbow. I'm shaking now, not sure what's wrong with me. I stutter, trying to find words, making old movements that no longer make sense, like tucking long hair behind my ear. There's nothing to tuck, so my fingers flail before I forget and shake out my hands mumbling something unintelligible along the lines of, "This was a bad idea. I can't—I—"

Chase nods as if he understands and slips away from me, taking his warm certainty with him. He places his hand on the doorknob and moves away from me as he opens the little door. "It's shock," he pauses and shakes his head once, foolishly, "I'm sorry, I don't know your name. If I unsettle you, we should call someone else, but you shouldn't be alone tonight. The hospital isn't far from here. Let me drive you. They can stitch you up and call your family."

I shake my head once, sharply. "No. No hospitals."

They'll run me through their system and suddenly every Ferro alive will know where I'm hiding. I swallow hard and keep my eyes fixed on the thick pine slats on the floor. I could call Lizzie. She'd be here in a few hours if she took the Ferro jet. No one would stop her. She could be in the air before my parents realized it. My eyes shift back and forth, thinking. I wanted to be left alone for a while, until I knew what to do. Involving more people puts everyone at risk. I can't do that to her. I shouldn't do it to Chase either.

He nods solemnly in front of the open door as if he understands. Folding those strong arms over his chest, he suggests, "A friend, then?"

"No." I shake my head and walk toward the couch, barely two steps away from the door and flop down onto the violet fabric. Chills overtake me and I shudder violently. What the hell is happening? Why am I shaking so much? I've done worse, lived through horrible things, and this never happened to me before.

I feel his eyes on me, a sympathetic gaze that would condemn me as soon as he realizes who I really am and what I've done. He's a good man, I can see that even through this frozen haze of fear. It licks at my skin, freezing my bones, and edging me too close to crying. I tighten my stomach and swallow the sobs but I'm racing the clock.

Chase moves slightly, his fingertips caressing the stubble on the hard angle of his jaw. Then he taps his cheek with his index finger, glancing at me while he does it. "I can't leave you alone. It would be incredibly cruel. You have no reason to trust me, but I won't give you a reason to hate me. Listen, I'll get you something to eat and you can try to lie down. I'll stay on the deck and you can lock the door, but I'll be here if you need me. Don't ask me to leave you alone, because I don't think I can be that bastard. Not tonight."

When I glance up, our eyes lock. The softness that emerged earlier is back and pleading with me. It's a look of empathy that I won't receive if he figures things out, and this is a smart man—he will figure it out. But not overnight. And not from the porch.

I find myself nodding slowly, shivering. I wrap my arms around my middle and hold on tight, but it doesn't stop. Coldness wraps it's icy grip around my shoulders and slithers down my spine. I can't chase it away.

Chase clears his throat from the doorway. "I'm going to get you something to eat and find a blanket. Can I come in?"

I laugh at the absurdity of it, joking to take the concerned look off his face. I hate feeling broken. "Are you a vampire? Do I seriously need to give you permission?"

I'm shaking, holding myself together with my arms and failing. Every shallow stitch, every weak binding, is under pressure and ready to tear apart. Tears sting my eyes and I no longer blink them away. Instead, I lean forward and let my eyes close as I press my forehead to my knees. It's better to hide behind snarky comments and shock than deal with the shit-storm headed my way. I gasp as another shiver rakes my spine.

"Where are your blankets?" I hear him ask urgently, and when I don't reply he's up the ladder and into the loft. Suddenly my bedspread is around my shoulders and tugged tightly under my neck. His hand is on my back as he whispers in my ear, "Sit up a little and hold onto this. Keep talking."

I sit up a little and take the blanket, clutching it under my chin. I don't lift my gaze. This feels too much like failure. I should never have to rely on anyone like this, never mind a stranger. "Are you this nice to all the girls who Taze you?"

He snorts. "Only the chicks who do it more than once. They need to be committed, you know?"

"Committed to an asylum? That's your type? Or are you talking about dedication?"

"Ah, isn't that the question?" Chase is in my slim fridge pulling out bottles and packages. I have no idea what he's doing because I can't seem to focus. "I suspect the voltage is the real attraction. Getting Tazed makes me hot."

I bark out a laugh unexpectedly, and tease, "That's sexy."

Chase glances at me from the kitchen counter, two steps away, those blue eyes filled with concern and concealed by a smirk. He's me. The way he hides his emotions, the way he doesn't respond or does the most preposterous thing. Something taught him to deflect people the way I do, but he's not bitter about it. He's not afraid.

He shrugs and goes back to piling a bunch of meat on a piece of bread. "I can't deny who I am any longer. I admit it, I was prowling that bar and picking fights hoping to get juiced. You made my night, Weird Girl."

Snorting, I smile and lift my face. "I'm not the weird one here."

He finishes stacking the sandwich, grabs a can of soda from the fridge, and walks toward me with a towering plate of food. "You're not? I thought for sure that you'd be the odd duck out of the two of us?" He hands me the mini buffet piled on the plate and then leans against the wall opposite me.

"Why's that?" I take a bite of the monster sandwich. It's not until after I've swallowed that I realize I would have never taken food from a stranger under normal circumstances. He could have poisoned me, put a shiv in the bread, or done any number of things to harm me.

Growing up in New York does things to a girl. The women down here don't think like that. They don't naturally distrust people to the same extent. Yeah, they look under the stall door in the ladies' room at a gas station, but the assumed animosity and distrust of other people aren't there. I feel foolish doubting him. Why would he save me, help me, and then poison me? Maybe I am mental.

He lifts a hand toward me. "Well, look at you. The Crayola hair and the piercings. I bet you have a tattoo hidden somewhere as well." The corner of his mouth lifts. "What does it say? A poem is my guess."

I frown as I take another bite and chomp, oddly unself-conscious in the moment. "It's not a poem."

A beautiful smirk. He unfolds his arms, slipping his hands into his pockets. "So a quote, then? Something that justifies your actions while conveying something you strive toward. Let me think. What could it be?"

I don't tell him he's right. There's no way he'll see the tat anyway. I crunch on a pickle and offer him the other. "Seriously, take it. Eat something. I feel weird eating alone." It's the truth.

He watches me carefully before taking the pickle from my hand. Our fingertips touch for a moment and a warm jolt races up my arm. It's like static, almost. Not a hot jolt of lightening, but a warm, steady surge of something. My brain isn't working. I blink and touch my head with my forefinger and thumb, squeezing my temples.

"Headache?"

I nod. "Yeah, it's not that bad."

"Finish eating and try to lie down for a while. Nothing will hurt you while I'm here. And you know you're in Texas now. If that asshole finds you and takes a step on your property, you have every right to shoot his ass." Chase is serious and he assumes I have a distaste of pain, of weapons, and wouldn't do it.

The truth is I've done so much worse, and without justification.

"I mean it," he pauses again and laughs. "I keep going to say your name, but you still haven't told me."

I don't want to lie to him. There's something about him that warns me not to do it. I stand and take a step toward him. "I don't want to talk anymore tonight."

The man is a breath away. His gaze lingers on mine as he breathes. Each pull of air fills his lungs, expanding his chest so that he's a fraction of a centimeter from touching me. I can feel his warmth, his concern. He wants to save me, but no one can. I've done this to myself and once everything catches up with me, my life is over. I never told Lizzie, because I could barely admit it to myself, but I'm not going back home. My life ended that night. There's no going back and the future that lies ahead is bleak and unforgiving.

The solitude of it scares me. Maybe that's why I ask, otherwise, I don't know what possesses me to suggest it. "Will you hold me for a while? I'm still shivering a little."

Chase swallows so hard I can see it in his throat. The

Adam's apple bobs up and down as he silently nods. I slip my hand in his, shut the front door as we pass by, and stop before the ladder.

I drop his hand and look back at him. "You don't have to —I feel bad asking. You've already done enough. More than I deserve."

"Kindness is something to spread. It's not anything owed or required. I never expected to end the night in your bed. In fact, I shouldn't go up there." His brow is wrinkled and his lips press together tightly.

I nod tightly and swallow hard before forcing a smile. "I understand." As I turn away from him and grab the lower rung, I feel his hand on my shoulder.

"I don't think you do. You seem to think the world is tit for tat. It's not. If I don't show you that, then who will? It's not that I think you should be alone tonight. Under difference circumstances, I'd—"

I hold onto the rung, staring at the metal bar in my hands. "You'd what?"

"I'd jump at the chance to sleep with you. You're my type, Weird Girl. I think you're incredible, brave, and a little jaded. But you're not so bitter you can't laugh, not yet. I see you."

A shiver travels up my arms but it has nothing to do with shock this time. Staring at the rung, I say softly, "Bree. My name is Bree." I can't tell him who I really am, but I can tell him the name I've been going by down here.

I swear that I can hear him smile behind me. "Thank you, Bree. Maybe one day I'll discover your whole name, the middle one, too."

Smiling at the rungs, I nod. "Maybe." Glancing over my shoulder, I meet his gaze, adding with a playful smirk, "Maybe not."

CHAPTER 9

THREE DAYS LATER

*L*ying in my bed, I stare at the inky sky filled with wide brush strokes of glittering stars. Out of everything I ever wanted to own, to touch—that's it. The majestic splendor of it leaves me in awe every time I climb up here. There's nothing that compares to the way lying here in solitude makes me feel.

Well, that's not entirely true. That night began with a little ember of a thought that blossomed into a flame that flickers brightest in the dead of night when I'm alone. What if I had someone to share this with? What if Chase had followed me up here? 'What if' followed by 'what if.'

What if I wasn't a Ferro.

What if that night had never happened?

What if there were a way to move forward without scattering my ashes to the wind?

Too many questions and not enough answers. I did this to myself. I need to keep reminding myself of that. I've been played in the past, but not this time. It was solely my fault, my responsibility. Lizzie is buying me time so I can figure out what happened, because there are still parts I'm missing, things I don't know. That night doesn't make sense. It shouldn't have ended in a pool of blood, but it did.

I swallow hard and roll over. I've not left the house for three days. I called in sick to work so I wouldn't get fired, but that also means no internet. There's no way to know if my stalker is going to out me. So I remain hidden, biding time until I can figure out how to approach this mess.

Lifting my gaze, I peer through the glass once more, wishing I could escape all this and have the freedom I've always longed for. To not be a puppet or a pawn or a killer. One could only wish now. It's too late. And I'm selfish for not running Chase off. Okay, I tried to get rid of him, but he keeps coming around. I should have pulled out a shotgun and threatened him to get off my land. That would have been a clear message.

Instead, I tell him not to come, but he does and he brings breakfast every morning and dinner every night. He says it's only this once, that I shouldn't get used to it, but another day passes and the same scenario repeats. I look forward to that part of the day the most, and consider what it would be like if he came a little earlier or left a little later. Or if we were tangled together? Or if I used him the way I used so many other men and tossed them aside? I'm not the slut my parents believe me to be, but at some point sex detached from love, and I began to doubt that there was such a thing.

Chase nailed me on that point. I don't believe two people

can fall in love, not anymore. It's another myth, a fairytale for idealists who haven't yet lived life. They don't know how dark it can get, because if they did, they would see the folly in falling for anyone. Love is the fastest way to bring about heartache and demise. The premise is a trick, a trap for the weak and foolish. I cannot afford to be a fool. Never again will I have such a luxury.

CHAPTER 10

$\mathcal{I}$ hear Chase's motorcycle before I see him riding down the gravel road toward my house. It's set back from the road, so the little path looks like it leads nowhere, like so many roads around these parts. Some are there for hunters to use to access blinds, while others are for farm owners to easily cross their property on ATVs. The tiny path that leads to my tiny home is unassuming. It's not until you round a corner about half a mile back from the road that you see the clearing with the little home.

Chase cuts the engine and dismounts from his bike. It's still early and the sky is yet to streak with pink and gold like spilled paint. I watch him tug his full face helmet off and rest it on the seat of the bike before opening the saddle bags to pull out two white sacks with a golden M on the side.

Perched on my elbows, I wait to watch him stride toward the door. I wonder what he's thinking, why he's decided to watch out for me, because that's the clear impression he's given. He thinks I'm alone in this world and believes that no one should be so secluded. At least that's what I tell myself.

The other option is that he really does get off on being Tased and is hoping for another jolt.

I snort a laugh, watching from the thin upper window of the house. Chase runs his hand through his dark hair as he turns toward the door. Two steps in and he glances up before he sees me. I go rigid and feel my face catch fire before slinking down out of the window, feeling sheepish. I tug on an oversized sweatshirt over my bra and panties, before descending the rungs.

Padding toward the door, I yank it open already saying, "I wasn't watching you, so you can stop smirking like you're God's gift."

His smirk only gets bigger. He hands me a bag and keeps the other for himself. "Whatever you say, Bree." He unfolds the tiny table that folds into the wall and then slips into the seat he staked out a few days ago. "Besides, I can't fault you if you like what you see." He unwraps his sandwich without looking up at me.

I grab the only chair in the house and plop down my bag of food on the table. When I sit, my shirt rises a little and covers my upper thighs, but I still have to pay attention to how I move and not bend over. I don't want him to think I'm easy. For once, that reputation isn't here and I don't want it to return. Not with him.

His gaze drops to my thigh and the long stretch of pale skin that connects somewhere under the giant shirt.

"Hmm, same here." I lift an eyebrow when he glances at me, startled.

Chase clears his throat. "Sorry. Leg man. I thought you'd wear pants or shorts or something." He avoids my gaze for a moment and clears his throat. "I can buy you some."

My jaw drops, as does my egg sandwich. "I own pants!"

"Yeah?"

"Yes!"

"So you just don't wear them, then?" He bites into his breakfast and acts like this is normal breakfast chatter.

"It's my house. I can't run my air conditioning all the time. You're lucky I have a shirt on at all. It's hot in here." I grab the neck of the sweatshirt and tug it, allowing it fall back in place and bringing a nice breeze.

"That'll teach me to bring a beautiful woman breakfast, me showing up and finding you naked in bed, ogling me out the window."

I frown. Okay, it's a pout. "I wasn't naked."

He arches a dark brow at me and tips his head my way. "Ah, but you were ogling me. Knew it."

"Ass." I smirk.

"I know you like it." He grins before meeting my gaze. "So, what plans do you have today? Besides hiding within the tiniest house in Texas?"

My stomach twists. I don't want to go into work and I'm too nervous to venture out. I shouldn't involve this guy. He needs to go. I turn on bitch mode and sniffle at him. "Nothing that concerns you. By the way, you shouldn't keep showing up unannounced. I might shoot you one day."

"And why would you do that?" He doesn't take offense and still has that chill banter thing I'm getting attached to.

Crank it up, Jos. Get rid of him. I lean back in my chair and fold my arms over my chest. "Because I got sick of seeing your ass on my property."

Chase leans in and says with a deep bedroom voice, "If that's what you want, Bree. I'll leave and never bother you again. Just say it. Look me in the eyes and tell me that's what you really want."

My inner bitch tumbles off her stilettos at the burst of candid honesty. He continues, "I'd like to take you out today, if that's okay with you. I have the day off and you could use a few laughs. It's up to you, although I think you should put some pants on before we go. Most of the guys around here aren't as open-minded as I am."

He flicks his blue eyes up and meets mine. Too soon, he turns away, grabs his trash and throws it away. He's at the door and I still haven't answered. He pulls it open and my heart sinks. He steps through the threshold and I can't breathe, my chest is so tight. I shouldn't speak. Stay silent, Jos. Don't say it. Let him walk away.

But I can't. Just before the door closes behind him, I shout out. "Wait, I'll put on pants."

FREE SAMPLE: HOT GUY

FREE SAMPLE

Turn the page to read a hot sample of a cool stand alone, big fat novel filled with banter and sexy fun!

CHAPTER 1

~AIDEN~

y heart slams into my chest like I'm having a fucking heart attack. I pull up Chad's number and press CALL. He's been my best friend since we were in boarding school together. I unload all my shit in the longest sentence ever heard. I don't fucking come up for air until I'm done. Panic has its icy fingers around my throat and I can't shake the bastard.

Chad's on speakerphone as I floor the sleek black McLaren across the Verrazano Bridge and toward eastern Long Island. I'm bobbing and weaving through traffic, gripping the wheel so tight that it might come off in my hands.

I rant for a while and then slam my palm into the steering wheel. "What the fuck am I going to do? I did every last fucking thing that man ever asked of me! I'm screwed, Chad!"

"I'll help you think of something. Don't worry. You got this." Chad gives me the pep talk I need as I drive away from Uncle James's swank office in Manhattan. "Go have a few drinks, nail some hot chick, and we'll work it out on paper tomorrow."

I grimace and stare at the dashboard, making the same expression I'd offer if Chad were here with me. "Tomorrow's Thanksgiving, asswipe. You're supposed to be at your mother's house."

He laughs lightly, "She can wait."

"She'll kill you." His mother is like Martha Stewart, pretrial, on crack. Their estate home on the north shore of Long Island is pristine and the holiday will be exceptional, until Chad shows up in jeans and a T-shirt instead of a tie. Formality isn't dead, not in that house.

"Fine, then come with me. Eat turkey, talk turkey, and then poke your eye out with the wishbone, because my fucking Hallmark family is *that* boring. We'll need some drama. If I have to sit through another holiday meal and listen to shit about hedge funds, I'll fucking snap." His voice rises an octave as he speaks so fast that all the words run together.

Chad's family has more money than God, but he doesn't act like it. Not until he's forced into the annual soul-sucking conversations about his future. When we were in college together, Chad nearly cracked from all the pressure put on him by his parents. Yeah, he has a set that's still married after thirty-five years, which is a feat in and of itself. At times, like holidays—like now, with all this shit raining down—it's difficult to not be envious. He has meddling parents. I have an evil uncle. That's it. No kin to call my own, no family watching my back come hell or high water. No cousins or brothers. Chad is my only family.

I assure him, "I'll go with you. Calm the fuck down. Hedge funds are better than this shit."

Chad laughs but there's no joy in it. "I'd trade lives with you in a fucking heartbeat, Aiden."

"Likewise buddy," and I mean it, "but first, I need to get through this shit."

"Tomorrow, Aiden." He urges. "Tonight, let your subconscious do all the thinking. Actually, let your dick do all the thinking. Pound some pussy and get smashed, in that order. It'll give you something to be thankful for tomorrow." Chad laughs and disconnects.

I sigh and rub my hand over my face. It's not a bad plan, but I feel too wound up for it. I'm still pissed. By now I've driven so far out on the Island that I'm passing the county line into Suffolk. Shit. It's another hour to the summer house and an hour back to the city. When I took off, I was irate and started to drive without thinking about where I was going. All I could focus on was finding Ocean Parkway and letting the salty sea air fill my lungs as I gunned it down the road.

I groan and glance around. I left the Parkway behind a while ago, and am flying down an open stretch of Sunrise—a modest concrete wonder with six lanes that connects suburbia to the city. Buildings jut up from the landscape, nothing more than three stories. If you took Manhattan and tipped it over on its side, you'd have Long Island.

I drive like I have a destination in mind. I don't want to go to the normal places tonight. I can't face those people. They all know who I am, what I am. If they find out what happened, I won't be able to bear it.

I drive a bit further and stop just outside of Bayshore, past the mall, in a sketchy part of town. I roll into the back parking lot of a bar and cut the engine. I strip off my jacket and tug on an old gray sweater I left laying on the passenger seat. It's old and soft. Combined with a pair of shitkickers, I know I can handle myself.

When I walk into the establishment, I'm thinking bar fight. That's why I stopped here. I need to beat the shit out of someone, and lose the anger building inside of me. This gutter looks like the perfect place to do it. But then, I spot this blonde in the corner with her nose in a book. Long tendrils of golden hair fall over her shoulders. Her face is perfect, fucking beautiful, not that I look at it too long because her tits are there in this red ribbed sweater, plump and perfect. I can imagine my hands on them as I kiss her senseless, spread her legs, and fuck her until she cries out in ecstasy.

I walk over to her and stop in front of her table. She's reading a Chilton's manual, which shocks the hell out of me. I pull out a well-worn wooden chair and sit without asking. "Light reading?"

She doesn't glance up at me, just gives me the finger. "Fuck off, buddy. I'm not in the mood." Her petite face remains downturned, her nose in that fat-ass book.

"Neither was I, until I saw you." That makes her look up. She stops for a second, startled. I think she recognizes me, but then her eyes tell another story—blank. She has no clue who I am, which is fucking perfect.

"Nice line. Use it often?" She smirks at me, lifts a brow, and then goes back to her book, turns a page. She opens the index and goes to a previous section and then pinches the bridge of her nose like she has a massive headache. I say nothing, and just watch her for a second. The manual is for Hondas that are over a decade old. I saw one in the parking lot on the way in.

I reach across, and take the book from her even though I know she'll rip my arms off. "Hey!" She reaches to take it back, and I grab her hands and squeeze hard before releasing them. I push the book back at her.

"Listen, I've had a shitty day and from the way you're flipping through the pages of that manual, you're stuck here until you can get your car to start. Honda Civic, am I right?"

She frowns and her lip juts out. It's so fucking perfect. I want to lean in and taste her, suck that pouty lip into my mouth and nip her.

Her gaze narrows. "How'd you know that?"

I run my hands through my hair and then lean on my elbows, getting closer to her. Her scent fills my head—fuck, she's intoxicating. "Listen, I'll fix your car and then you can spend the night doing funner things, or you can stay here alone. Up to you."

She hesitates. "What do you know about cars?"

I don't answer her. Instead, I get up and tip my head toward the door. "Keys?"

She stiffens, and then sighs as she reaches into a purse that looks like a horse-feed bag. She fishes them out and hands them to me. "Fine, but if you steal my car, I'll kick your ass."

I smirk at her. I like the spunky thing she has going on. This chick isn't a pushover, which means she should be a lot of fun in bed. I offer a lazy smile and lean in close, invading her space and inhaling the perfect scent. "Tell me, honey, how exactly would I swipe a car that doesn't run?"

Her eyes lock with mine. Defiant. "You'd be surprised at what a desperate guy is willing to do."

I choke and laugh at her. "Desperate? That's what you see when you look at this?"

She shrugs and gives me a once over, folding her arms loosely over her chest. She stands on one leg, which tips her curvy hips to the side, and glares at me, like she's bored. "Does it matter?"

I step closer, her body an inch from mine. I can feel the warmth of her body. She's close enough to touch, but I'm having too much fun taunting her. I feel the words wrap around my lips as I say them. "Desperation and kindness don't mingle."

She snaps, and lunges for the keys. "I don't need charity."

I pull back, letting her body brush against my arm. I hold the keys out of reach and look down into her beautiful face.

There's something about her that's so different. I honestly think she may knee me in the nuts, take back her keys, and figure out the Chilton's manual. "Good, because I'm not offering a handout. I never said I was paying, honey."

Her gaze narrows. "Stop calling me that."

"What? Honey? You're not all sweet and smooth, going down?"

She snorts. "Well, you'll never find out, will you?" She raises her brows at me and smirks.

Holy fuck. I love this woman. I can't believe she said that. I lean in close enough to see the tiny freckle that rests on the soft skin just above the bow in her top lip. She stiffens and lowers her lashes, her gaze fixated on my mouth thinking that I'm going to kiss her.

Instead, I stop and whisper as I grin. "Stop thinking about it."

"I'm not," she breathes, but I know she is from the way her gaze drops. She doesn't move. She stays there a breath away. When she shifts her weight, her tits brush against my chest. It's enough to make me want to take her here and now. "Besides, certain acts are reserved for men who are worth it, and you're questionable at best."

"Then, I'll have to change your mind."

She smiles and watches me from under those long lashes. "Once I form an opinion, it doesn't change." Her minty breath washes across my lips as she speaks. It's fucking hypnotic.

"Then, I'll be sure to leave you with a lasting impression—something unforgettable." I turn on my heel before she can say another word, or change her mind, and head toward the door. She follows me out into the parking lot.

I pop her hood, the real one, but see the problem as soon as I sit down behind the wheel. It's basic, but not something that I can fix in a parking lot. I try to crank the engine. It doesn't even sputter and I point to the dash. "See that needle?"

"Yeah, what about it?"

"It means your battery is dead."

"But I just changed it. It's new. It can't be dead."

"Odds are it's your alternator, but someone needs to check it out. A jump won't bring this battery back to life. Hell, it's so far gone that the dome light isn't even coming on"

She inhales slowly, doesn't blink, and then swears under her breath. Hand to her head she says, "Shit. I can't fix that myself." Her book has black smudges and oily fingerprints all over it. I have no doubt that she's been working on the car.

"Not tonight, but given enough time in the light of day, I'm sure you could figure it out." I mean every word of it. There's something about her, I can see it in her eyes. She likes to tinker, to take things apart and put them back together. She's not a grease monkey—it's more than that. It has something to do with curiosity and understanding. She wants to know how things work.

She softens a little. "Thanks. I think I'm going back to plan A for tonight."

"Which was…?"

Her green gaze cuts to the side, landing on me. "Getting plastered and joining AAA so they can tow my car home."

"As amazing as that sounds, I can have your car fixed in a couple of hours. It'd be ready for you, right here. And I can't help but notice there's a nice warm room right over there." I tip my head at the little Hilton glowing in the cold night. She's shivering, no coat, and doesn't flat out reject me this time. "Which would you prefer? Drinking buddy or getting off with a guy who can make a girl come three times, back to back? It's pretty amazing, at least that's what I've been told." I hold her gaze, shocked she hasn't shot me down yet.

She rolls her eyes and tries not to smile. Tucking a piece of hair behind her ear, she glances up at me. "You don't need to hype yourself. I'm not blind."

"It's not hype. It's a fact, and I felt like you needed the choice. But it is fucking cold out here, so how about picking one. Either way, I'll make sure you forget everything that's bothering you for a little bit. What do you say?"

She sighs loudly and looks back at the bar. She's going to pick drinking buddy. Her body language says it all. Slumped shoulders, apprehension, lack of trust. She's strung tight like she might punch me in the face for the hell of it.

Then she looks down at my hand and takes it, threading my fingers through hers. "Grab a bottle to go, and let's get the hell out of here."

CHAPTER 2

~AIDEN~

*T*have no idea who this woman is and I don't ask her name. She doesn't ask for mine. I grab a bottle of Absolute and check in under an alias, pushing the guy at the desk a hundred when he wants to see my license. He takes it, and suddenly that part isn't important anymore. It's amazing what people will do for a few bucks at this time of year.

A nervous energy radiates from the blonde goddess standing next to me. Her body is tense, all lean muscle, and she's strong. I got that. She's not a doormat and sure as hell doesn't take shit from anyone. I wonder how crazy she is for a second, eyeing that massive purse, knowing damn well she might be insane. There could be an ax in there. The hot ones are always nuts.

Hot Girl follows me to the room and when we walk inside, I flip on the lights. I toss my keycard on the cheap counter and look at the sad little room. The bedspread has that once white look and the room is well lived in. I'm about to turn around and tell her that she doesn't have to do shit with me, that we can drink in here—I'm fine with it—when she shuts the lights off and steps toward me with a look in her eye that's all sex.

She wants me, is thinking about clawing her nails down my back and riding my dick. I wonder if she wants me or just needs an escape. It doesn't matter, not tonight. Her arms are around my neck and her perfect little body presses against mine. Her tits mash against my chest making my dick hard. She smells like vanilla and baby powder. Coupled with that peppermint breath, I could eat her up. Her hair feels like silk in my fingers and when her lips meet my neck, she trails her hands up under my sweater running her palms over my abs slowly, teasing me.

She breathes into my ear, "Open the bottle and let's get to it."

"Anything you want." I crack open the vodka and ask if she wants ice, but she shakes her head.

"Neat is fine." She downs the first cup and then a second one before tugging that sweater over her head. She steps toward me with her golden hair tossed over her shoulders and a black bra that makes her tits look better than the sweater. It's not fucking possible to look at her face when she's this hot. The best part, she has no fucking clue. This chick probably thinks she's cute or pretty. She has no idea that guys like me fantasize about a body like this. She's curvy with a narrow waist and her hips spill down into thighs that I can't wait to get between. She's a fucking seductress with a fairy's face and a saunter that would make a succubus jealous. The girl's got moves.

She pulls my sweater over my head and walks around me slowly, dragging the pads of her fingers across my stomach, side, and then across my lower back. She stops behind me and presses her tits to my back, rocking those sweet hips toward me. I feel her hot kiss on my skin and it takes every-thing I have to stay still and see how this plays out. Most women wait for me to make the first move. I can count on one hand how many times a woman has controlled me in bed. Most don't even try.

She places a palm on both sides of my waist and asks, "Why aren't you drinking?"

"I thought you'd have a better time if I wasn't totally plastered."

"Plastered would be bad, but a little tipsy might be fun. Take a drink." She releases me and then walks over to the bed, sits down on the edge and crosses her jean-clad legs at the knee. She leans back on her arms which pushes her chest out, making her body look even more appealing.

She doesn't have to ask me twice. I pour a double and down it fast, before walking over to her. I'm about to push her back onto the bed when she stops me, grabs my waist-band, and unbuttons my jeans. The zipper slides down slowly as she watches with fascination. I feel her hand wrap around my shaft and swallow a moan. She smiles as she feels its girth, squeezing me firmly, making me harder, longer with her touch. She slides down my jeans and strips my boxers, leaving me naked and standing in front of her, my erection before her eyes.

She glances up at me from under her lashes. "Is anything off the table?"

Oh fucking hell. She's perfect. I shake my head. "You?"

"No." She takes a swig from the bottle.

I do the same before putting it on the nightstand and lying back against the pillows. I lace my arms behind my head. I glance at her and see her eyes on my face, questions fade when she kneels on the bed and unhooks her bra. She tosses it to the side, and I can see the swell of her tits and those nipples, tight and perfect for me.

I grin at her and command, "Strip. Lose it. All of it."

She doesn't speak, doesn't play coy, or act shy. She obeys

and it makes me hard again. The way she slips out of her jeans and panties, she tosses them aside without a drop of shame and waits. I could learn to enjoy this. She goes from being in charge to being compliant. I want to feel her naked body pressed to mine.

Before I can act, there's a knock at the door. I look at Hot Girl for a second and she says, "Go ahead and answer it. I'm not going anywhere." She leans back against the pillows.

I'm torn, I don't want to leave her—not even for a second —but the asshole is knocking more urgently now. I swear and grab my jeans, pulling them on fast, and then pull on my shirt. I walk over to the door and yank it open. When I see who's there, I step into the hallway, closing the door behind me.

Chad is grinning. "Lovely place to spend the night."

I glare at him and hiss, "What the hell are you doing here?"

"Saving your ass. Come on. I stumbled on something, but it'll be gone by morning."

I glance at the door. "I can't walk out on her. She'll never forgive me."

Chad scoffs, "You'll never see her again. Your ass is on the line. Fix it and then nail some other girl. She's a piece of ass, they're all the same."

He sounds completely reasonable, but in the back of my mind, I know this one is different. If I leave now, I shoot any chance I have of being with her to hell.

Chad tugs at me. "Come on. We're running out of time. We have to get there before the shredding company."

"Where are we going?"

"Norvek." The company that should have been mine. The company I nearly bankrupted. "It could save your ass."

I walk away from the woman on the other side of the door without an explanation.

CHAPTER 3

~KRIS~

I tug my long hair over my shoulder, away from my sweaty skin, and smile. He's insanely hot. In fact, I could have fallen for him and I know it. To save myself the heartache, I took him to bed. At least that's what I tell myself as I wait for him to come back. There's no way to recover from a one-night tryst with a random guy. I've tried it. There's nothing after that which could possibly live up to the unrealistic expectations that have grown in my mind. If a guy is good in bed, he's usually a total asshole, which is why I had a long string of non-serious relationships until I met Carl. As for the one-nighter type of men, their bedroom skills come from years of dicking around, nailing anything that moves. This guy has mad skills, but there's something else there—a haunted look in his eyes.

Something is gnawing away at him. I sense it, I'm not sure what it is exactly, but the slope of his shoulders and the twinge of regret in his voice makes me wonder. Maybe he's coming off a bad break up too. Or maybe he just doesn't want to be alone. Night is the worst time to be isolated.

Every worry I ever had seems to creep up until there's no escape. Being alone makes it worse.

I don't want to think of Carl or what happened. There's a hole in my chest where my heart belongs. Easing the ache for a bit, a distraction of slick bodies and sensations will help. It helped in the past, but the effects don't last long enough. I thought I was done with this part of my life. It's strange to be back in this vulnerable spot. Maybe I use sex as a defensive mechanism, a way to push guys away. The truth is, I didn't plan on stopping at the bar tonight. The day went to hell and the car died just as I ran off from Carl. Luckily, I was able to push it into the nearest parking lot, which was the bar across the street. No one stopped to help, not that anyone ever does. It's not like that here. At this point, my car is mostly duct tape and barely runs, but it's all I have.

I know what I'm doing is reactionary. That if I hadn't gotten dumped, I wouldn't have said yes to this guy. Add up the rejection, cheating, and disbelief and I want to forget for a while. I can't believe Carl was seeing someone else while he was living with me. I can't get past that. What's wrong with me? How did I miss that?

Then I quit. I walked away from a great job. I had no choice. I can't go back there.

I'll have to visit the employment agency on Friday and beg for a shit job that pays too little. People ask me why I'm not in college, or they look at me and assume I'm a student. It makes job-hunting difficult. I'm a social pariah for not continuing my education. There's so much pressure to do what other people think is right. At times, I'm not sure who I am at all. Add in the swiftly approaching holidays and this entire mess is a nightmare. I don't want to think about Thanksgiving tomorrow. I don't want to pretend that it won't suck, that I'm fine. I'm not, but I can put blinders on and keep marching.

One day everything will be all right. One day things will be good again. Until then, keep going and don't stop. If I slow down, I'll fall apart. I can't let that happen.

I'm twirling my finger against the sheet forcing my mind back to thinking about the stranger. His body tells me everything I need to know. He's a pampered ass, one of those rich kids that has time to work out and get rock hard abs and a matching ass. His arms are thick, powerful, but he's careful with me. I like it. I can't wait to see what he's going to do.

I roll onto my side after a second. I glance at the door that hasn't moved. The hallway is silent. His sweater is still on the chair. The pit of my stomach dips. There's no way he walked out, but the sinking feeling in my gut is telling me a different story. I wait another minute or two and pull on a robe and pad over to the door. I press my ear to the door and listen.

Nothing.

I pull the door open wide, throwing it back, hoping he's there, but the hallway is empty.

CLICK HERE TO CONTINUE READING HOT GUY.

COMPLETED SERIES BY H.M. WARD

ROMANCE

~SECRETS & LIES~

~STRIPPED~

~THE PROPOSITION~

~DAMAGED~

~LIFE BEFORE DAMAGED~

~SECRETS~

~SECRET LIFE OF TRYSTAN SCOTT~

~SCANDALOUS~

TEEN PARANORMAL

~DEMON KISSED~

Please turn the page for a suggested reading order.

SUGGESTED FERRO READING ORDER

THE ARRANGEMENT 1

THE ARRANGEMENT 2

THE ARRANGEMENT 3

THE ARRANGEMENT 4

THE ARRANGEMENT 5

THE ARRANGEMENT 6

DAMAGED 1

DAMAGED 2

SECRET LIFE OF TRYSTAN SCOTT 1

SECRET LIFE OF TRYSTAN SCOTT 2

SECRET LIFE OF TRYSTAN SCOTT 3

SECRET LIFE OF TRYSTAN SCOTT 4

SECRET LIFE OF TRYSTAN SCOTT 5

THE ARRANGEMENT 7

THE ARRANGEMENT 8

THE ARRANGEMENT 9

THE ARRANGEMENT 10

THE ARRANGEMENT 11

SCANDALOUS 1

SCANDALOUS 2

STRIPPED 1

THE PROPOSITION 1

THE PROPOSITION 2

THE PROPOSITION 3

MORE BOOKS BY H.M. WARD

SCANDALOUS

SECRETS

COLLIDE: THE SECRET LIFE OF TRYSTAN SCOTT

DEMON KISSED

CHRISTMAS KISSES

OVER YOU

HOT GUY

And more.

To see a full book list, please visit:

www.hmward.com/BOOKS

CAN'T WAIT FOR H.M. WARD'S NEXT STEAMY BOOK?

Let her know by leaving stars and telling her what you liked about this book in a review!

ABOUT THE AUTHOR

New York Times bestselling author H.M. Ward continues to reign as the queen of independent publishing. She surpassed 13 MILLION copies sold, placing her among the literary titans. Articles pertaining to Ward's success have appeared in The New York Times, USA Today, and Forbes to name a few. This native New Yorker resides in Texas with her family, where she enjoys working on her next book.

You can interact with this bestselling author at:

www.hmward.com

Made in the USA
Columbia, SC
18 June 2017